THE SANTA FE JAIL

LARS JAKOBSEN

GRAPHIC UNIVERSE™ • MINNEAPOLIS • NEW YORK

FOREWORD

THE HISTORY OF OUR WORLD IS BEING REWRITTEN, BUT NOBODY KNOWS IT...YET!

A NEW TECHNOLOGY HAS BEEN DEVELOPED BY A SMALL TEAM OF SCIENTISTS. ONE OF MANKIND'S BIGGEST DREAMS HAS BEEN ACHIEVED: IT IS NOW POSSIBLE TO TRAVEL IN TIME.

THIS TECHNOLOGICAL MARVEL, CALLED THE TIME GUN, HAS FALLEN INTO THE WRONG HANDS. SECRET AGENTS FROM ALL OVER THE WORLD ARE FIGHTING A NEW AND DANGEROUS CRIME WAVE.

THESE AGENTS ARE RESPONSIBLE FOR KEEPING HISTORY IN THE RIGHT ORDER AND ENSURING THAT VALUABLE ARTIFACTS ARE NOT REMOVED FROM THEIR OWN TIME.

BUT TIME TRAVEL HAS ITS LIMITS... IT IS NOT POSSIBLE TO CHANGE YOUR OWN DESTINY. EVERY LIVING PERSON HAS A BEGINNING AND AN END THAT CANNOT BE REWRITTEN. WHO KNOWS, MAYBE YOUR NEXT-DOOR NEIGHBOR WAS BORN IN 1929 AND IS NOW 21 YEARS OLD.

AT THE SAME TIME
IN LONDON...

CHECKMATE,
LORD
GUINNESS!

?!?

YOU PLAY VERY WELL, MR. MORTENSEN. NOW TELL ME, HAVE YOU CONSIDERED OUR OFFER? WE NEED WILLIAM DELIVERED TO SAFETY. THIS IS A VERY IMPORTANT ASSIGNMENT.

SOMETHING TO DRINK, SIR?

!

MY MAID, RUTH. WE CAN SPEAK FREELY. SHE HAS MY TRUST.

I CAN'T TAKE THE JOB, MY LORD.

BUT WE WILL PAY ANY PRICE!

MR. MORTENSEN, MY ORGANIZATION HAS BEEN HUNTING A MYSTERIOUS AFRICAN METAL SINCE 1925. IT IS PRICELESS, BEYOND RARE. PERHAPS YOU'VE HEARD THE RUMORS?

GO ON...

LAST WEEK WE WERE CONTACTED BY A SELLER IN KRAKOW, POLAND. THE SELLER CLAIMS TO POSSESS THIS METAL.

WHAT DOES THAT HAVE TO DO WITH WILLIAM JENSEN?

IS THIS PRECIOUS METAL THE REASON YOU'RE SO EAGER TO PAY A MILLION-DOLLAR RANSOM?

!

WILLIAM HAS STUDIED THIS METAL. WE NEED HIS EXPERTISE TO VERIFY THE PURCHASE.

IS THIS ABOUT SAVING DR. JENSEN'S LIFE OR YOUR PRECIOUS BUSINESS DEAL?

DON'T MISUNDERSTAND. WILLIAM IS VERY DEAR TO US! HE MUST BE RESCUED!

ON THAT MUCH, WE CAN AGREE. WILLIAM NEEDS MY HELP.

CAN I TAKE THAT AS A YES?

I DON'T CARE ABOUT YOUR HIGH STAKES DEAL. BUT I'LL BRING DR. JENSEN HOME.

THE EXCHANGE WILL OCCUR AT THE OLD JAILHOUSE IN SANTA FE.

WE HAVE BURIED THE RANSOM IN THE DESERT NEARBY. YOU'LL DELIVER THE MAP TO THE KIDNAPPER AND BRING BACK WILLIAM. UNDERSTOOD?

I'LL DELIVER YOUR MAP, BUT THE REST IS UP TO YOU!

ONE HOUR TILL WE LAND IN SANTA FE...

MORE APRICOT JUICE, SIR?

THANKS.

HMM, AN ARTICLE ON THE BLACK CRUISE.

Winther&Co.

The Black C

By Kathryn Olsen

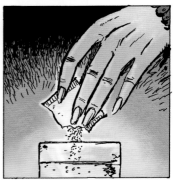

HE FAINTED! IS HE ALL RIGHT?

HE DOESN'T LOOK SO GOOD...

DON'T WORRY ABOUT HIM, HE ALWAYS GETS LIKE THIS WHEN WE FLY.

I'LL JUST TAKE THAT MAP, MR. MORTENSEN!

YOUR CARGO BOX IS READY, MA'AM.

THANKS! DON'T MIND MY HUSBAND. FLYING MAKES HIM SLEEPY.

THANKS TO YOU, I CAN RETIRE EARLY. HA! MAYBE I'LL HIRE A MAID OF MY OWN.

WHAT AWFUL WEATHER. I CAN'T SEE A THING!

I COULD USE A SWIG OF MIRACLE TONIC.

NOW WHERE IS AFRICA ON THIS MAP?

THESE ROAD MAPS ARE USELESS! I'VE GOT TO STOP BUYING MY MAPS AT THE GAS STATION.

HUH?

UH...WHERE AM I?

WHO ARE YOU? TRYING TO STEAL MY MIRACLE TONIC, I BET!

PCE F

?!

7

BUDAPEST 1901

MMM! GOOD COFFEE, RIGHT, BETH?

WHAT DID YOU FIND OUT ABOUT WILLIAM?

YOU REALLY SHOULD ENJOY ALL THE EXCELLENT COFFEE THAT 1901 HAS TO OFFER.

I DON'T PAY YOU TO DRINK COFFEE! WHERE IS MY HUSBAND?

RELAX, MY DEAR BETH. WE'LL FIND WILLIAM, DON'T YOU WORRY!

I'VE DONE MY JOB ALREADY. JUST WAIT AND SEE!

NOWADAYS, KIDNAPPERS CAN HIDE PEOPLE BY TRAPPING THEM IN A TIME THEY CAN'T ESCAPE FROM.

BUT THE KIDNAPPERS...WILL THEY HURT HIM?

DON'T WORRY ABOUT THEM. THEY'RE LONG GONE.

WILLIAM IS ALL ALONE.

NOW FOLLOW ME. WE'RE GOING TO MARGARET ISLAND.

ARE YOU GOING TO TELL ME WHAT WE'RE DOING THERE?

WE HAVE AN APPOINTMENT WITH YOUR HUSBAND!

THE ENGINE JUST DIED! THIS HAS NEVER HAPPENED BEFORE! WHAT ROTTEN LUCK!

BUT...

WE HAVE TO LAND THIS THING. WE CAN'T FLY WITH ONE ENGINE.

AND WHO ARE YOU?

WE'RE LOSING ALTITUDE! WHERE DO YOU KEEP THE PARACHUTES?

MIRACLE TONIC, DON'T FAIL ME NOW!

MAYBE THIS BATCH OF TONIC HAS GONE BAD...

COME ON! THE OTHER ENGINE JUST OVERHEATED. WE CAN'T LAND. WE HAVE TO JUMP!

OH MY!

TAKE THE PARACHUTE. WE'RE JUMPING NOW!

TODAY JUST ISN'T MY DAY!

OK, WHAT DO I DO NOW?

I HAVE A SUGGESTION...

GET ME DOWN FROM HERE!

LET'S START MOVING BEFORE IT GETS DARK. MAYBE WE CAN FIND SOME CIVILIZATION, SOMEWHERE.

LET'S EACH HAVE A GULP OF *MIRACLE TONIC!* IT MAKES YOU STRONG AS AN OX AND WISE AS A SAGE!

MIRACLE TONIC, HUH?

MADE FROM GINGER, SARSAPARILLA, AND JUST ONE DROP OF RATTLESNAKE OIL!

IT'S MY JOB TO DELIVER IT ALL OVER THE WORLD.

AND JUST HOW DID I GET INSIDE A CRATE OF MIRACLE TONIC?

!

A WOMAN SAID IT WAS A SPECIAL SHIPMENT OF TONIC HEADING TO THE SAHARA DESERT...

A WOMAN?

SHE WAS REAL PRETTY, BUT I DON'T REMEMBER HER NAME...

WHOEVER SHE WAS, SHE TOOK MY MAP.

WELL, WE SURVIVED A PLANE CRASH. WHAT ELSE COULD GO WRONG?

AHEM!

BACK IN BUDAPEST...

WILLIAM? IS THAT YOU?

SO...

THE SANTA FE JAIL, AT LAST!

WE PICKED A BAD PLACE TO HANG OUT!

MY NAME'S MORTENSEN, BY THE WAY!

GORDON!

HOW ARE WE GOING TO GET OUT OF THIS, GORDON?

I CAN'T THINK CLEARLY UPSIDE DOWN!

SSSH!

SO...

WHAT DID I TELL YOU?

BUT...BUT HOW?

SORRY TO TROUBLE YOU, DEAR. I HOPE YOU DIDN'T WORRY TOO MUCH...

WORRY? YOU WERE KIDNAPPED, THAT'S ALL! WHAT HAPPENED?

THE KIDNAPPERS ABANDONED ME HERE IN 1901, WITHOUT A TIME GUN. I HAD NO WAY TO ESCAPE...

BUT WHY? WHAT DID THEY WANT?

AND...

MORTENSEN'S IN FOR A SURPRISE. I LEFT THAT SCIENTIST TO ROT IN 1901.

NOW ALL I NEED TO DO IS WAIT.

I HAVE ALL THE TIME IN THE WORLD...

THE NATIVES CAN BE A LITTLE UNFRIENDLY.

WE JUST DISCOVERED!

AH, THAT'S BETTER!

LET'S GET OUT OF HERE!

MY NAME IS KATHRYN.

HELP ME WITH THIS CAMOUFLAGE.

SOME TONIC WILL GIVE ME STRENGTH!

THANKS FOR SAVING US!

DON'T MENTION IT. I COULD USE A BIT OF EXCITEMENT!

I'VE BEEN ON MY OWN FOR MONTHS.

WHAT ARE YOU DOING, ALONE IN THE JUNGLE?

WRRRRR

I AM STUDYING AN ABANDONED MINE. I'LL TAKE YOU THERE!

TONIC, ANYONE? I AM JUST DYING OF THIRST!

NO THANKS.

WE'RE A LITTLE LOST. PERHAPS YOU CAN TELL US WHERE WE'VE LANDED.

WE ARE IN THE IRINGA REGION OF TANZANIA, CLOSE TO AMELIA BAY. THE MINE ISN'T FAR FROM HERE.

SO WHAT KIND OF MINE ARE YOU EXPLORING?

I WISH I KNEW!

?

I WAS DOING SOME RESEARCH ON THE OLD BLACK CRUISE EXPEDITION. I FOUND SOME OLD GEOLOGICAL SAMPLES FROM 1925.

THEY WERE SO UNUSUAL. I JUST HAD TO COME TO IRINGA TO FIND THIS MINE!

WE'RE HERE! THERE'S THE OLD MINE.

WHO DO YOU WORK FOR?

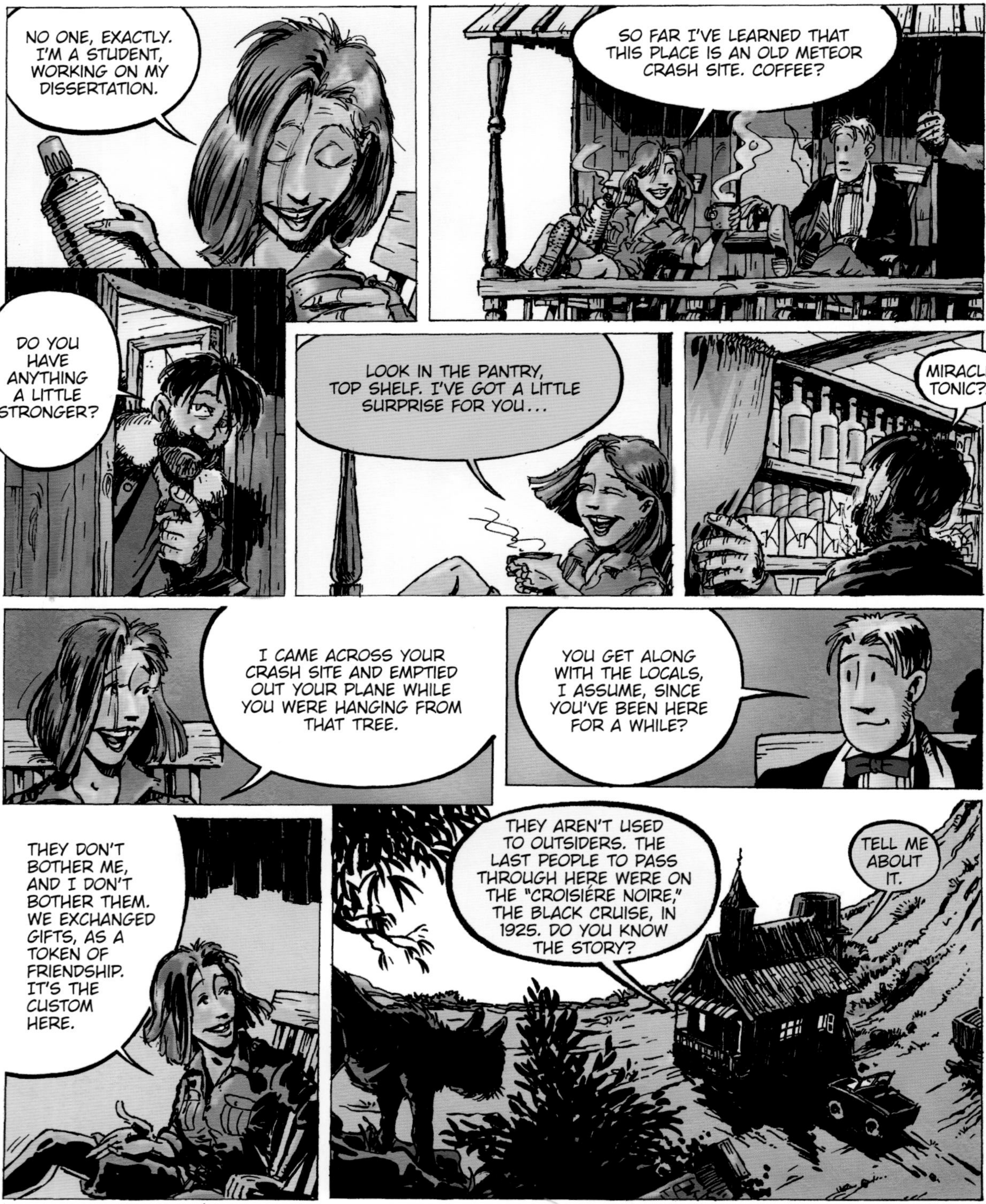
NO ONE, EXACTLY. I'M A STUDENT, WORKING ON MY DISSERTATION.
SO FAR I'VE LEARNED THAT THIS PLACE IS AN OLD METEOR CRASH SITE. COFFEE?
DO YOU HAVE ANYTHING A LITTLE STRONGER?
LOOK IN THE PANTRY, TOP SHELF. I'VE GOT A LITTLE SURPRISE FOR YOU...
MIRACLE TONIC?!
I CAME ACROSS YOUR CRASH SITE AND EMPTIED OUT YOUR PLANE WHILE YOU WERE HANGING FROM THAT TREE.
YOU GET ALONG WITH THE LOCALS, I ASSUME, SINCE YOU'VE BEEN HERE FOR A WHILE?
THEY DON'T BOTHER ME, AND I DON'T BOTHER THEM. WE EXCHANGED GIFTS, AS A TOKEN OF FRIENDSHIP. IT'S THE CUSTOM HERE.
THEY AREN'T USED TO OUTSIDERS. THE LAST PEOPLE TO PASS THROUGH HERE WERE ON THE "CROISIÉRE NOIRE," THE BLACK CRUISE, IN 1925. DO YOU KNOW THE STORY?
TELL ME ABOUT IT.

THE BLACK CRUISE WAS AN EXPEDITION ACROSS AFRICA BY CAR...

...LONG BEFORE THERE WERE MANY ROADS!

WHAT IS ALL THIS?

THIS IS MY RESEARCH MATERIAL ON THE BLACK CRUISE AND THE OLD MINE. THERE MUST BE A CONNECTION...

HMM...

HERE'S MY LATEST GIFT FROM THE LOCALS, WANT TO SEE? IT'S STRANGE...

IT'S SOME OLD CONTRAPTION.

SOMETHING IS VERY WRONG HERE!

I BET SOMEONE, SOMEWHERE, IS LOOKING FOR THIS! I NEED TO GET TO THE BOTTOM OF THIS.

OH!

MEET ME AT AMELIA BAY IN TWO DAYS!

IRINGA 1925

SO YOUR PLANE CRASHED?

I PUT ON MY PARACHUTE AND JUMPED!

WE WERE LUCKY TO FIND YOU! THESE JUNGLES CAN BE DANGEROUS.

HERE'S THE MINE. LET'S STOP FOR TODAY AND MAKE CAMP.

IT WAS CLOSED A COUPLE OF YEARS AGO. WE PROMISED TO BRING SOME SAMPLES HOME...

TIME FOR A FAMILY PHOTO!

MAYBE THIS WILL BE IN THE PAPERS SOMEDAY!

BLITZ

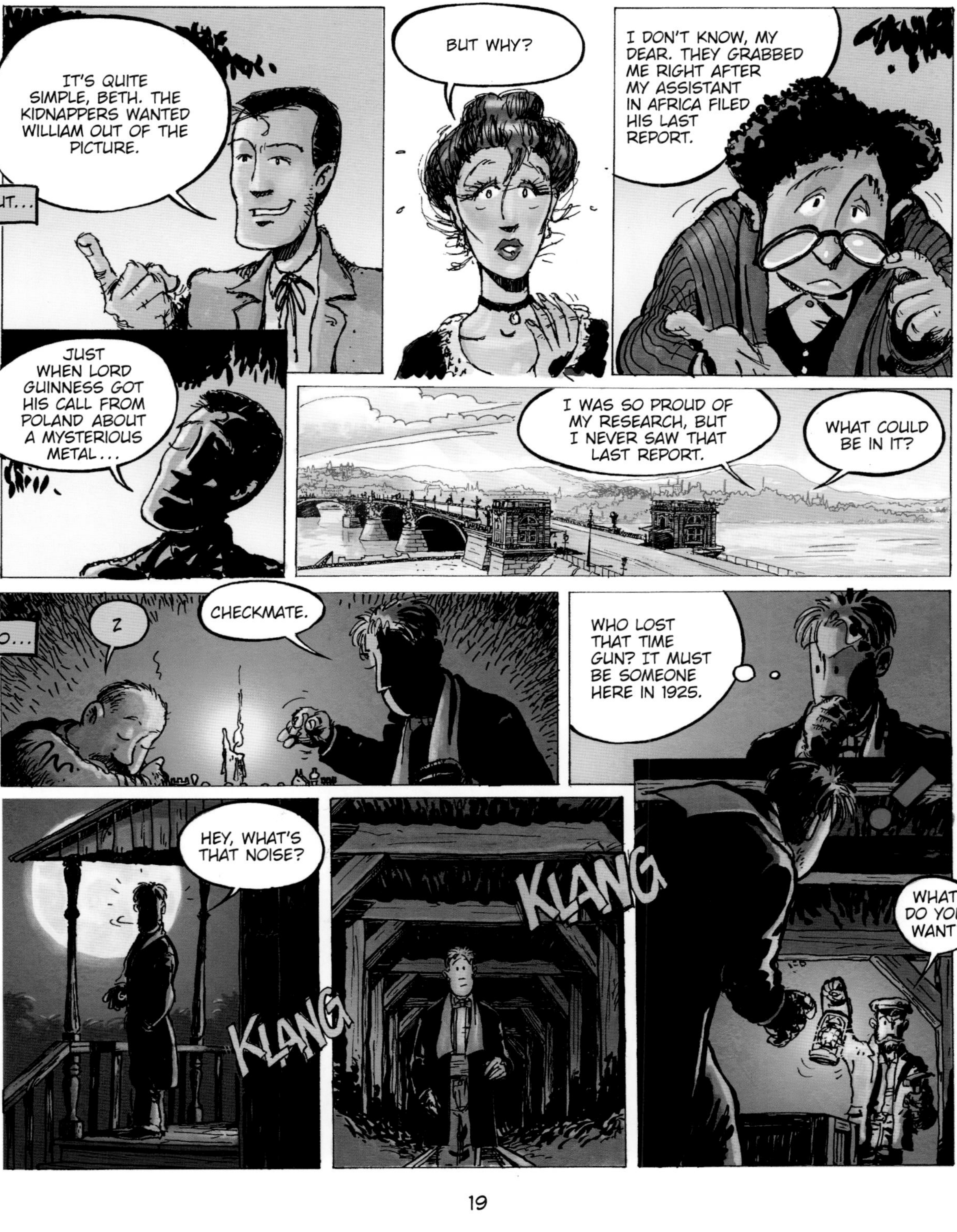
BUT...
IT'S QUITE SIMPLE, BETH. THE KIDNAPPERS WANTED WILLIAM OUT OF THE PICTURE.
BUT WHY?
I DON'T KNOW, MY DEAR. THEY GRABBED ME RIGHT AFTER MY ASSISTANT IN AFRICA FILED HIS LAST REPORT.
JUST WHEN LORD GUINNESS GOT HIS CALL FROM POLAND ABOUT A MYSTERIOUS METAL...
I WAS SO PROUD OF MY RESEARCH, BUT I NEVER SAW THAT LAST REPORT.
WHAT COULD BE IN IT?
SO...
Z
CHECKMATE.
WHO LOST THAT TIME GUN? IT MUST BE SOMEONE HERE IN 1925.
HEY, WHAT'S THAT NOISE?
KLANG
KLANG
WHAT DO YOU WANT?

AND...

I WAS CAPTURED RIGHT AFTER THE REPORT WAS SENT TO NOVA KRAKOV, THE METAL FOUNDRY IN KRAKOW.

I THINK THEY WANTED TO MAKE A DEAL WITH LORD GUINNESS WITHOUT ANY INTERFERENCE FROM ME.

SIMPLE, HUH?

BUT WHY?

THE ANSWER IS IN THE REPORT, I AM SURE!

AND WHERE IS THIS REPORT?

POLAND, 1973!

BY THE WAY, HOW DID YOU FIND ME?

THE NAME IS AGENT COOP. IT WAS QUITE SIMPLE, REALLY. YOU CHECKED INTO THE *GRAND HOTEL ROYAL* IN BUDAPEST ON APRIL 6, 1901.

HOW DID YOU KNOW THAT?

THE RECEPTIONIST TOOK HIS PASSPORT. I FOUND IT IN 1973, FILED UNDER "MISSING PERSONS." THE PAPERWORK LED ME HERE.

MAYBE YOU CAN HELP ME SOLVE ANOTHER MYSTERY...

WE'RE GOING TO POLAND!

SO...

AND WHAT ARE YOU LOOKING FOR?

NONE OF YOUR BUSINESS! GET LOST. I'M IN ENOUGH TROUBLE AS IT IS!

TELL ME WHAT'S GOING ON HERE!

YOU WOULDN'T BE LOOKING FOR THIS?

MY TIME GUN! BUT HOW?

I'M COLLECTING METAL SAMPLES FOR A SCIENTIST BACK HOME...

RIGHT. AND THE SCIENTIST?

HE'S A RESEARCHER WORKING IN BERLIN.

WHAT'S HIS NAME?

WILLIAM JENSEN.

IS WILLIAM BEHIND THIS?

DO YOU KNOW WILLIAM?

HE'S BEEN KIDNAPPED. I'M TRYING TO RESCUE HIM!

THIS IS ALL VERY STRANGE...

I WAS SUPPOSED TO EXCHANGE THE RANSOM IN SANTA FE IN 1973, BUT THINGS GOT OUT OF HAND...

YOU'RE IN THE WRONG TIME AND PLACE!

YES.

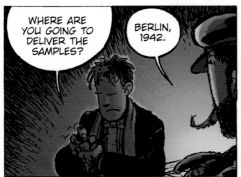

WHERE ARE YOU GOING TO DELIVER THE SAMPLES?

BERLIN, 1942.

IS WILLIAM WORKING FOR *THE NAZIS*?

I AM AFRAID MOST SCIENTISTS ARE FORCED TO, IN OUR TIME.

BACK IN BUDAPEST...

SO...

HERE'S MY PLACE. I JUST NEED TO GET MY THINGS.

I'LL WAIT HERE.

I'D BETTER CHANGE FOR THE TRIP.

THOSE CLOTHES WILL NEVER DO IN 1973.

WHAT WILL WE FIND IN POLAND?

NOVA KRAKOV IS IN POLAND, YOU SEE. THEY HIRED ME TO STUDY THE METAL SAMPLES FROM AFRICA.

LET ME FIND YOU SOME CLOTHES.

MY ASSISTANT FROM IRINGA TOLD ME THAT I WOULD BE KIDNAPPED, BUT I DIDN'T KNOW WHEN...

NOW WE'LL CHEAT THEM.

UH, YES!

OR BY WHOM. IT SOUNDS AS IF NOVA KRAKOV WANTED ME OUT OF THE PICTURE. THEY LIE AND CHEAT.

SO...

WE'RE OFF! TO AMELIA BAY!

IT'S NICE TO BE MOVING AGAIN.

I HOPE YOU FIND A PLANE FOR AMERICA!

OUR GEOLOGIST IS ALSO LEAVING US.

HE SAID THE BLACK CRUISE WILL BE A SUCCESS!

HE'S RIGHT!

ME TOO!

...AND SOON YOU WILL BE DEAD, MR. MORTENSEN!

YOU CANNOT SURVIVE MY ATTACK!

CHECK AND MATE, MR. LOUIS!

KRAKOW 1973

TRAIN NO. 26 WILL TAKE US TO NOVA KRAKOV.

WE NEED TO FIND THE COMPANY ARCHIVE.

THEN WHAT?

WE STEAL THE REPORT, OF COURSE!

I'M CURIOUS ABOUT WHAT IT MIGHT SAY. IT MAY EXPLAIN A GREAT DEAL...

WE'LL SAY WE ARE FROM THE BOARD OF TRUSTEES AND BETH IS OUR SECRETARY.

I HEAR THE ARCHIVIST PLAYS EVERYTHING BY THE BOOK.

WE'LL SEE...

THE GENTLEMEN FROM THE BOARD OF TRUSTEES WOULD LIKE TO SEE THE IRINGA PROJECT REPORT, THANK YOU!

CODE WORD, PLEASE!

UM.

AND...

NOW, WHERE ARE THEY?

WELL, LET'S HAVE A LOOK AROUND...

WAITER, ANOTHER MIRACLE TONIC!

HELLO, GORDON!

MORTENSEN, MY FRIEND! YOU'RE HERE!

HELLO, GUYS!

ALL TOGETHER AGAIN. LET'S CELEBRATE!

EXCUSE ME, CAN I HAVE A LOOK AT THAT RESEARCH BOOK AGAIN?

SURE, HERE IT IS!

MY FRIENDS CAN BE VERY BORING. TELL ME, DO YOU PLAY CARDS?

WHAT HAPPENED TO THE MINE AFTER THE BLACK CRUISE?

ACCORDING TO SOME OLD NEWSPAPER CLIPPINGS, THE NAZIS TOOK OVER THE RESEARCH IN 1942. A VERY VALUABLE SAMPLE WAS TAKEN TO THE GERMAN HEADQUARTERS IN DENMARK. BUT IT WAS NEVER SEEN AGAIN!

I'VE SEARCHED THE MINE FOR MORE SAMPLES, BUT THERE'S NOTHING LEFT. THIS METAL IS RARER THAN RUBIES!

SO THEY WEREN'T ABLE TO PRODUCE MORE OF THIS METAL?

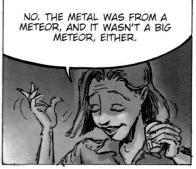

NO. THE METAL WAS FROM A METEOR, AND IT WASN'T A BIG METEOR, EITHER.

HMM...

HOW DID YOU GET HERE, BY THE WAY?

OH, I GOT A LIFT FROM A GUY IN THE JUNGLE.

JUST WHAT ARE YOU UP TO?

I'M JUST TRYING TO MAKE UP FOR LOST TIME.

WHATEVER YOU SAY! HERE'S MY ADDRESS. WHEN YOU GET HOME, DROP ME A LINE!

WHERE'S *GORDON?*

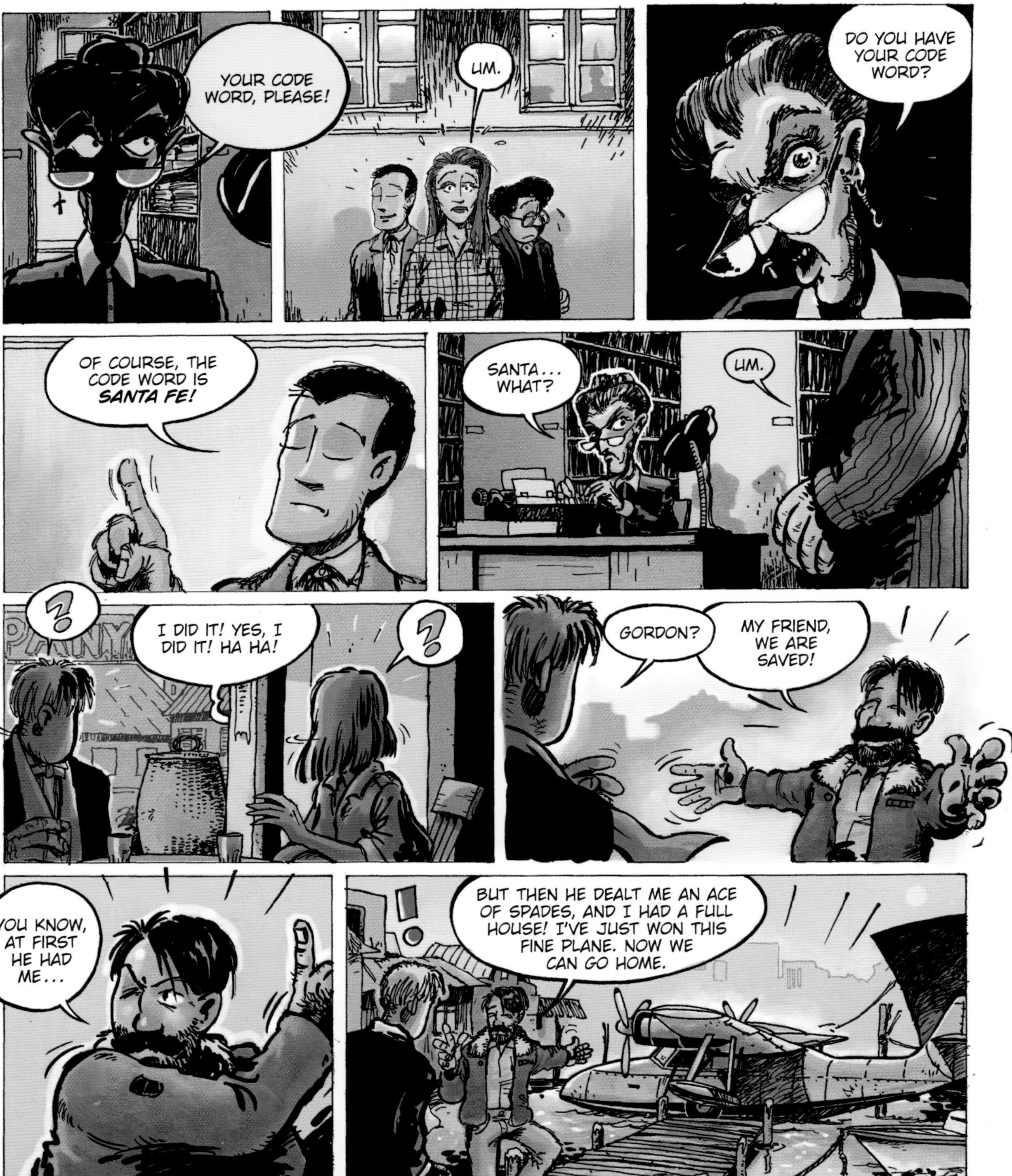
YOUR CODE WORD, PLEASE!
UM.
DO YOU HAVE YOUR CODE WORD?
OF COURSE, THE CODE WORD IS SANTA FE!
SANTA... WHAT?
UM.
?
I DID IT! YES, I DID IT! HA HA!
?
GORDON?
MY FRIEND, WE ARE SAVED!
YOU KNOW, AT FIRST HE HAD ME...
BUT THEN HE DEALT ME AN ACE OF SPADES, AND I HAD A FULL HOUSE! I'VE JUST WON THIS FINE PLANE. NOW WE CAN GO HOME.

SILKEBORG 1950

HERE I AM IN DENMARK.

THE NAZI HEADQUARTERS IN DENMARK WERE ABANDONED AFTER THE WAR ENDED IN 1945.

THE NAZIS WERE IN A HURRY TO LEAVE...

EVERYTHING WAS DESTROYED AND THROWN IN THIS LAKE.

NO VALUABLES WERE EVER FOUND.

WHAT'S THIS?

29

BURNED SLIDES?

A SOLDIER HOLDING A PAINTING... IT LOOKS VALUABLE.

IT WAS PROBABLY DESTROYED IN 1945 WHEN THE NAZIS SURRENDERED.

AND A SOLDIER HOLDING SILVER AND OTHER VALUABLES. THIS MUST BE PLUNDERED TREASURE.

AND THIS... AN OFFICE AND A RADIATOR?

WHY TAKE A PHOTO OF THIS?

EXCUSE ME, MR. MORTENSEN?

SORRY IF I DISTURBED YOU!

NOT AT ALL, BUT WHO ARE YOU?

MY NAME IS PROFESSOR STALITCNEYER!

SOONER OR LATER, YOU WERE MEANT TO COME BY THIS PLACE, AND I JUST LOVE TO TAKE MY AFTERNOON WALK AROUND HERE.

IT LOOKS AS IF YOU HAVE THE SITUATION UNDER CONTROL.

THANKS, BUT HOW DO YOU...

WILLIAM IS A DEAR FRIEND. WE DO APPRECIATE WHAT YOU ARE DOING FOR HIM.

WILLIAM?!

YES, WELL, I'VE GOTTEN A LITTLE OFF TRACK. I WAS HOPING I MIGHT FIND SOME CLUES HERE.

AND YOU...

WILLIAM IS OUR COLLEAGUE. HE HAS OUR DEEPEST RESPECT!

OUR?

WE ARE A GROUP OF UNIQUE GENTLEMEN WHO MEET OUTSIDE OF TIME, TO ENJOY ONE ANOTHER'S COMPANY.

AND WILLIAM?

WE'D LIKE TO OFFER HIM A PLACE IN OUR SECRET SOCIETY.

I HAVE TO FIND HIM FIRST.

YES, AND MAYBE YOU'LL STUMBLE OVER THE NAZIS' HIDDEN TREASURE?

I THINK THE TREASURE MIGHT BE THE SECRET METAL FROM IRINGA...

GOOD THINKING!

AND...

WILLIAM WAS KIDNAPPED BECAUSE NOVA KRAKOV DIDN'T WANT HIM TO INTERFERE WITH THEIR DEAL. THEY'RE TRYING TO SELL METAL THAT DOESN'T EXIST.

I DO HOPE YOU FIND WILLIAM. HERE'S OUR SECRET ADDRESS.

THANKS.

I THINK I ALREADY KNOW WHAT'S IN THE REPORT. THERE NEVER WAS ENOUGH METAL TO PUT INTO PRODUCTION.

I'M SURE THE METAL IS HERE SOMEWHERE.

WHERE COULD THE NAZIS HAVE HIDDEN IT?

AS SOON AS I FIND IT, I'M HEADING TO POLAND.

MAYBE I'LL FIND MY NEXT CLUE THERE.

SO...

SEE...NO PROBLEM!

NOW SIGN HERE AND USE YOUR PERSONAL STAMP!

STAMP?

WHERE DO YOU HIDE SECRET TREASURE?

YOU CAMOUFLAGE IT?

AND MAKE IT LOOK LIKE SOMETHING ORDINARY...

THE SLIDES MAY HELP. I NEED TO FIND THIS OFFICE.

THIS MUST BE IT...

OF COURSE!

NOW I KNOW WHAT TO DO!

KRAKOW 1973

33

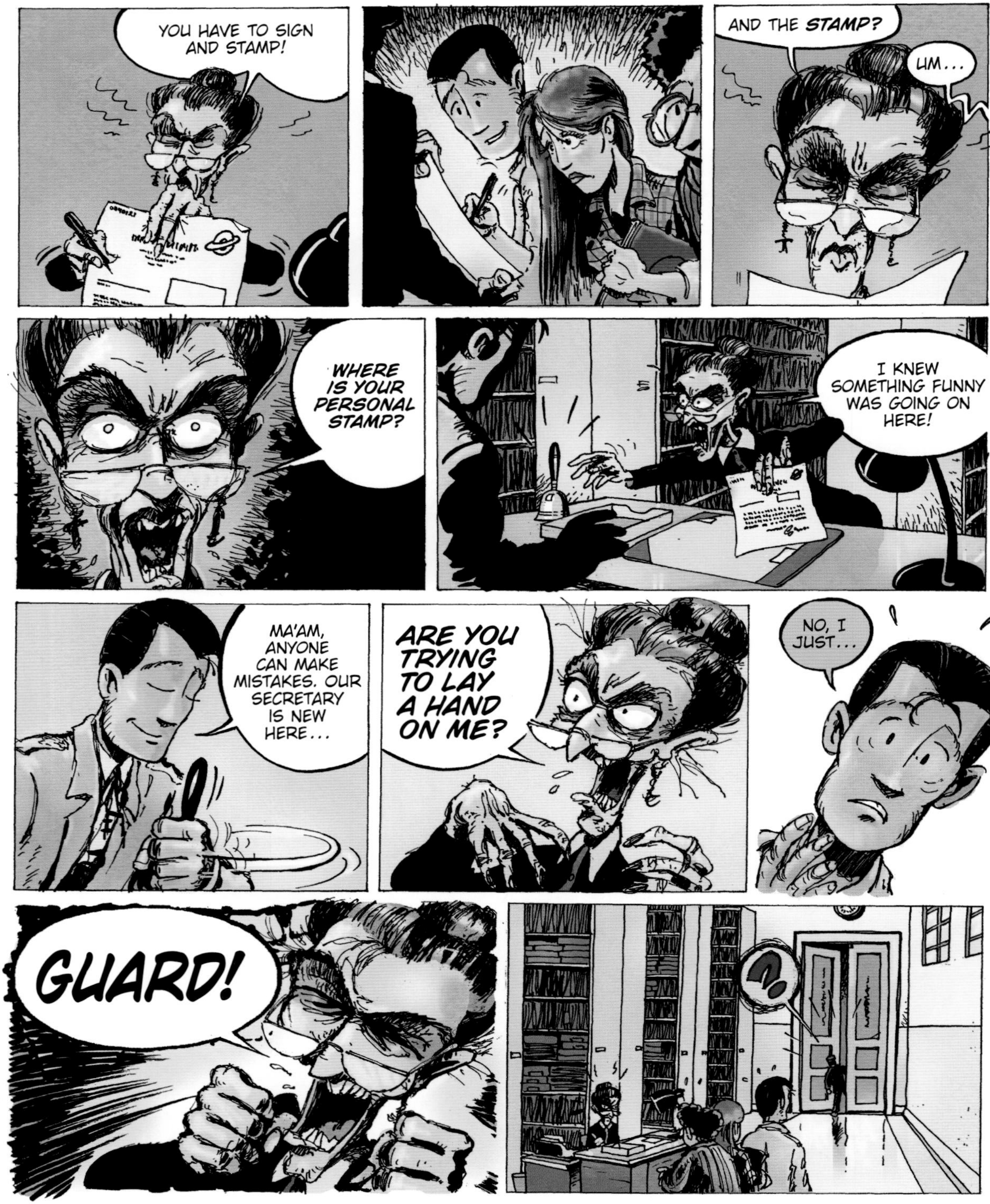

YOU HAVE TO SIGN AND STAMP!
AND THE STAMP?
UM...
WHERE IS YOUR PERSONAL STAMP?
I KNEW SOMETHING FUNNY WAS GOING ON HERE!
MA'AM, ANYONE CAN MAKE MISTAKES. OUR SECRETARY IS NEW HERE...
ARE YOU TRYING TO LAY A HAND ON ME?
NO, I JUST...
GUARD!

THEY ATTACKED ME AND DISTURBED MY WORK OF THE UTMOST IMPORTANCE. *SEIZE THEM!*

AT ONCE.

GOOD THING I SPOTTED THOSE IMPOSTORS.

WHERE ARE YOU TAKING US?

I'M TAKING YOU HOME, WILLIAM!

BUT...

POOR MORTENSEN, HE'LL NEVER SAVE THAT SCIENTIST NOW. THAT RANSOM IS ALL MINE... I JUST HAVE TO FIND IT FIRST!

35

FINALLY, WE MEET, DR. JENSEN. MY NAME IS MORTENSEN.

HUH?

I WAS HIRED TO DELIVER YOUR RANSOM AND BRING YOU HOME SAFELY, BUT YOU DON'T LOOK VERY KIDNAPPED TO ME...

NO, NOT EXACTLY. I WAS ABANDONED IN TIME, IN 1901. WE ARE TRYING TO GET TO THE BOTTOM OF THIS MYSTERY.

BUT WHAT ARE YOU DOING HERE?

WE TRIED TO FIND THE SECRET REPORT. MAYBE IT WILL HAVE SOME ANSWERS.

I CAN TELL YOU WHAT'S IN THE SECRET REPORT. THE METAL CAME FROM A SMALL METEORITE. THERE WAS NEVER ENOUGH TO PUT INTO PRODUCTION.

I'M SO SORRY FOR THE TROUBLE. ALL MY RESEARCH WAS FOR NOTHING...I HAVE NOTHING...

DEAR...

I'M NOT SO SURE, WILLIAM. I KNOW SOMEONE WHO WOULD LIKE TO MEET YOU...

THEY HID WILLIAM AWAY SO HE WOULDN'T LEARN THE TRUTH AND REPORT TO LORD GUINNESS.

36

HERE IT IS!

HERR STALITCNEYER.

?

MORTENSEN, WILLIAM! AND WHAT'S YOUR NAME, MY DEAR?

BETH.

COME ON IN, EVERYBODY. MEET THE GUYS...

HERE'S OUR LEAGUE OF EXTRAORDINARY SCIENTISTS!

YOU ARE WELCOME TO STAY!

THANKS, BUT I HAVE BUSINESS IN SANTA FE!

AND...

LORD GUINNESS SAID HIS MAID HAS GONE MISSING. SHE MUST BE AFTER THE RANSOM.

SHE MUST HAVE RENTED A CAR. MAYBE THIS PLACE...

RENT A CAR

FINALLY, A LEAD!

THEY SAY SHE JUST LEFT. SHE CAN'T BE FAR!

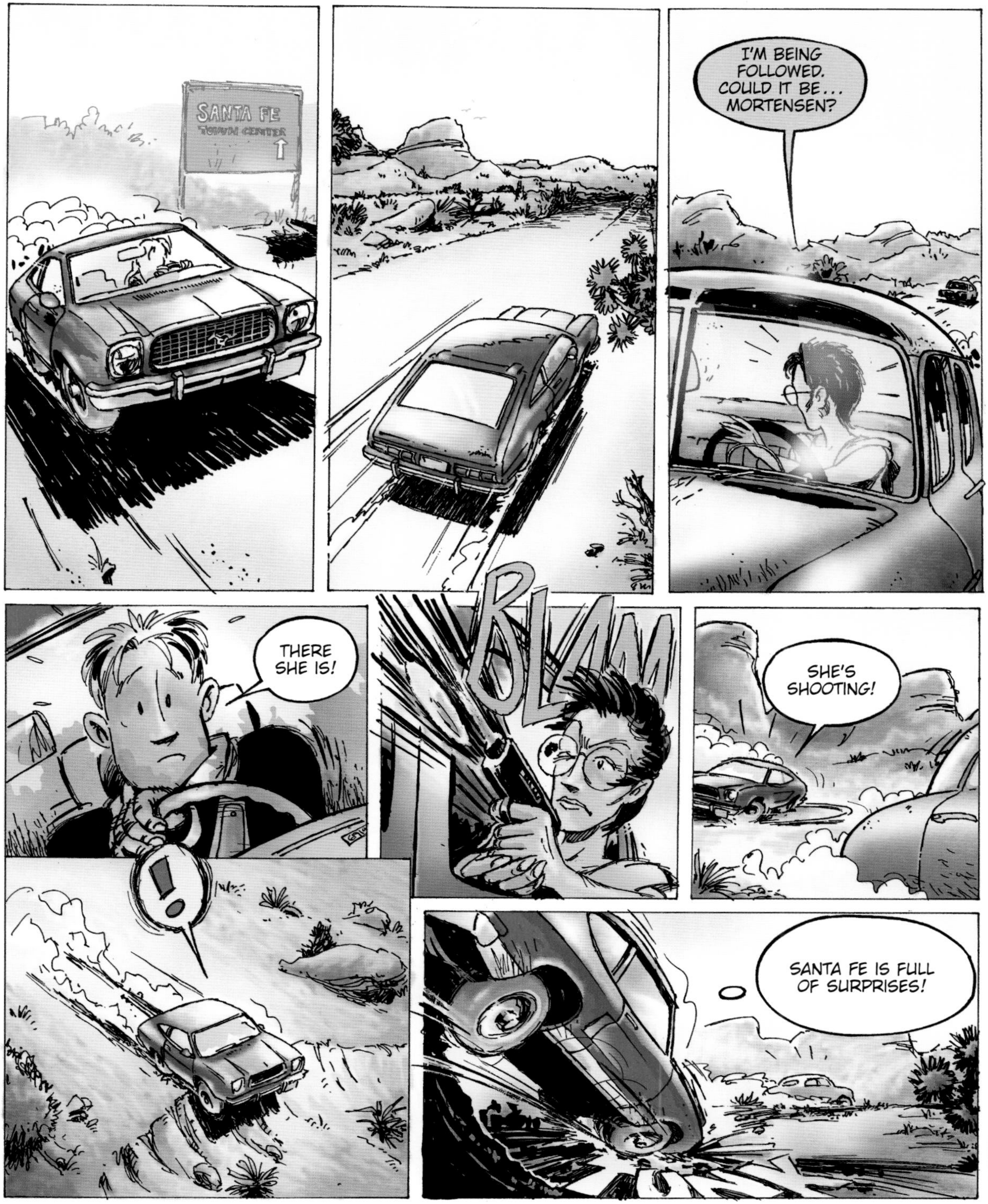
SANTA FE
TOWN CENTER
I'M BEING FOLLOWED. COULD IT BE... MORTENSEN?
THERE SHE IS!
BLAM
SHE'S SHOOTING!
!
SANTA FE IS FULL OF SURPRISES!

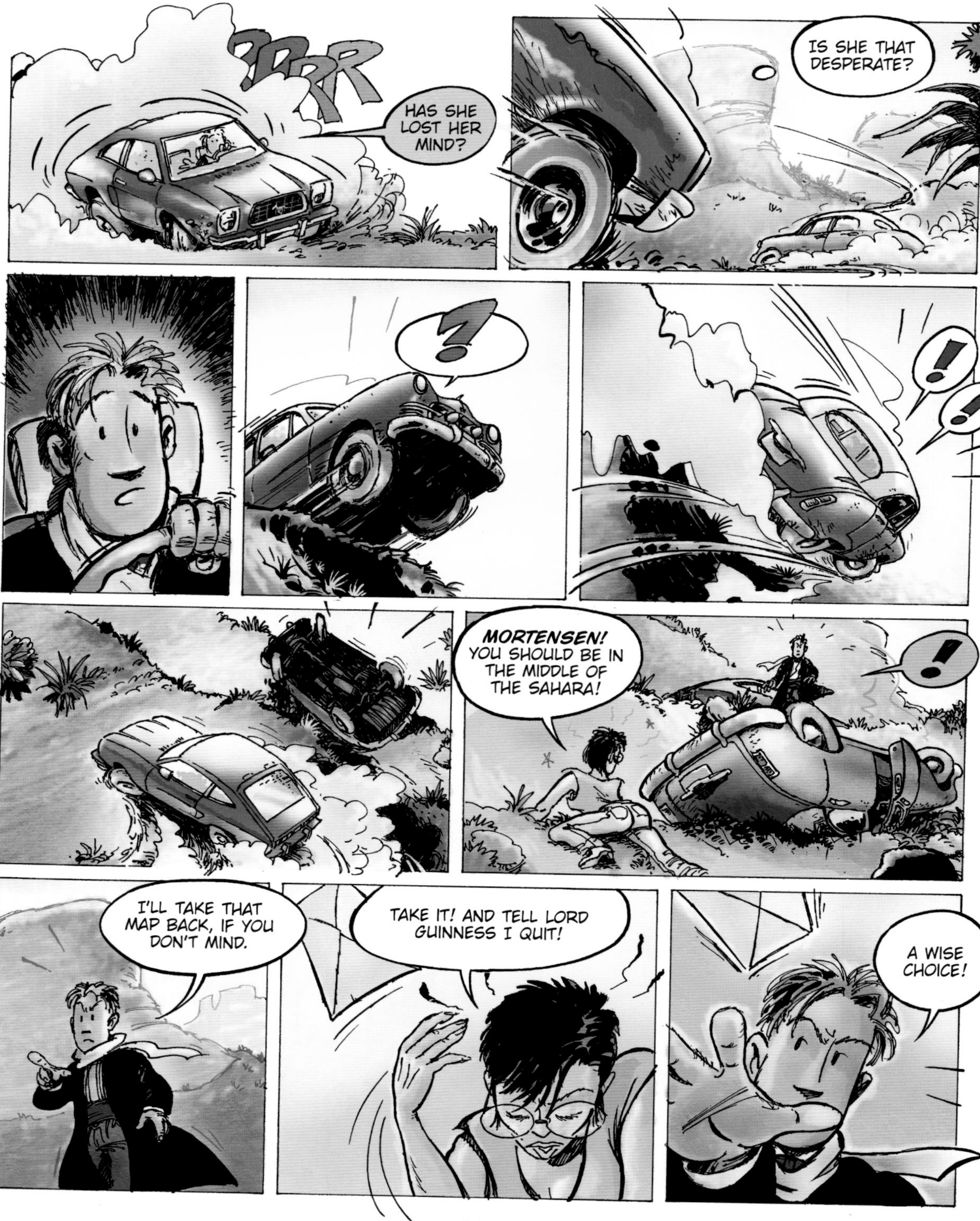

DRRR
HAS SHE LOST HER MIND?
IS SHE THAT DESPERATE?
?
!
!
MORTENSEN! YOU SHOULD BE IN THE MIDDLE OF THE SAHARA!
!
I'LL TAKE THAT MAP BACK, IF YOU DON'T MIND.
TAKE IT! AND TELL LORD GUINNESS I QUIT!
A WISE CHOICE!

AND NOW THE LAST STOP: THE SANTA FE JAIL!

THEY NEVER INTENDED TO RETURN WILLIAM. WHOEVER IS WAITING AT THE JAILHOUSE...

...IS PROBABLY PLANNING TO SHOOT ME AND COLLECT THE RANSOM.

WELL, WE'LL SEE WHO SHOOTS FIRST!

!

HAVE A NICE TRIP!

PHEW!

DRIIIII

DELIVERY! THIS PACKAGE HAS BEEN STORED FOR YOU IN OUR WAREHOUSE FOR OVER TWENTY YEARS!

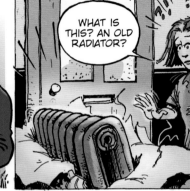

WHAT IS THIS? AN OLD RADIATOR?

HERE'S YOUR RANSOM BACK. I DIDN'T NEED IT AFTER ALL! WILLIAM IS SAFE.

WHERE IS HE? I'M ABOUT TO CLOSE THE DEAL!

THE DEAL IS A SCAM. BUT YOU'RE LUCKY, YOU DIDN'T LOSE A CENT. JUST A MAID.

HMPH.

PERHAPS I AM LUCKY, AT THAT. THANK YOU, MORTENSEN!

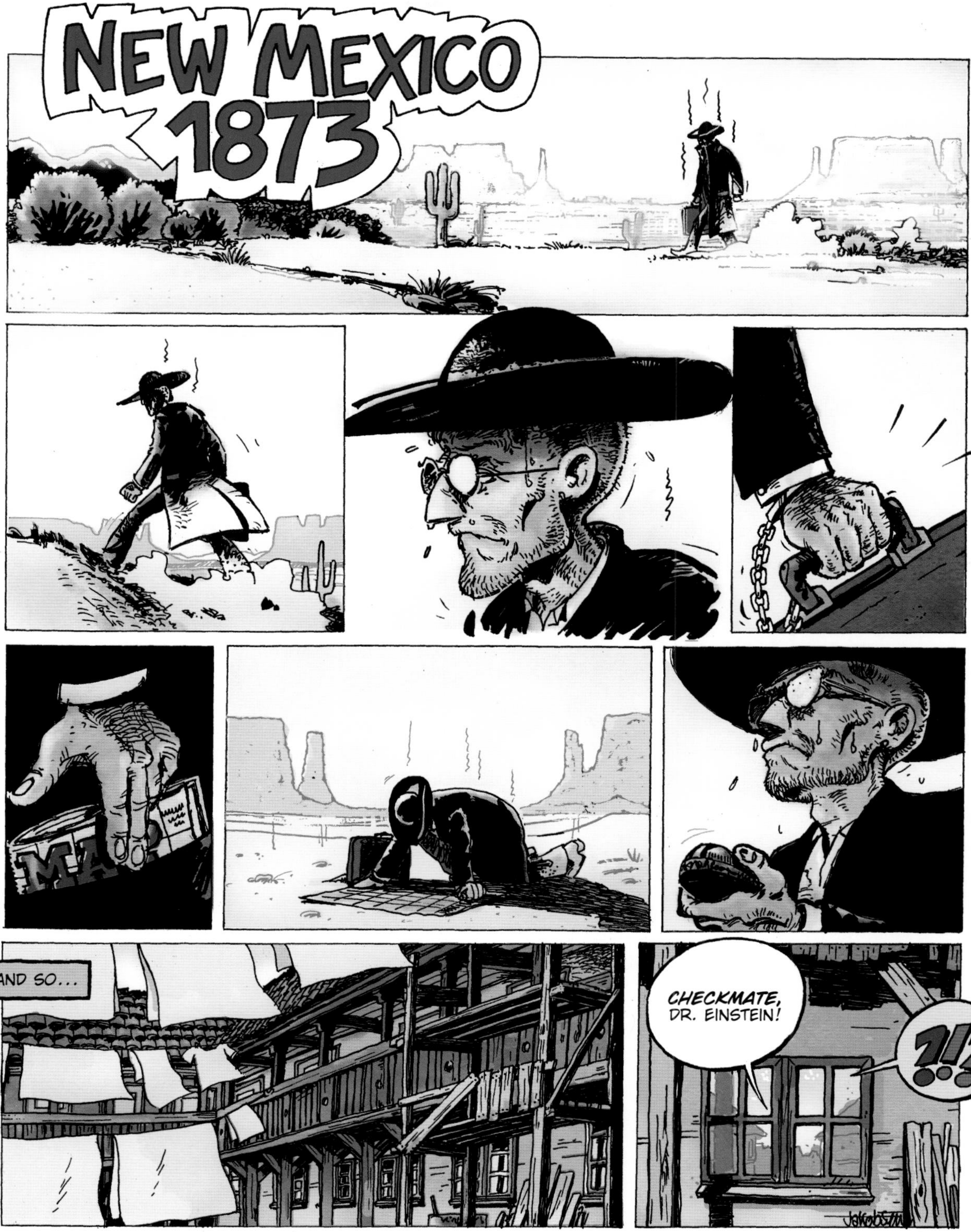
NEW MEXICO
1873
AND SO...
CHECKMATE, DR. EINSTEIN!
?!?

Jailhouses in the Old Days

Die Pillory Strafe

In colonial America, punishment for crimes was often severe and public. The whipping post and the pillory, a wooden frame that locked the head and hands in place, were used to punish offenses that would be considered minor misdeeds today, such as swearing, lying, or skipping church. Jails were only used for temporary stays for debtors, vagrants, and accused criminals as they awaited trial. After a trial, the prisoner was set free, punished, or executed.

As the population of the colonies grew, jails became more crowded. Jailers usually did not provide free food, clothing, or blankets—these necessities could be purchased from the sheriff. In Philadelphia's Old Stone Jail, the sheriff even provided a bar where prisoners could buy alcoholic drinks for inflated prices. Poor prisoners went hungry and became sick, and death was not uncommon.

After the American Revolution (1775–1783), Dr. Benjamin Rush, Benjamin Franklin, and other organizers fought to reform the criminal code. Rush believed that public punishment did not improve the criminals or decrease crime. He helped create reform measures that favored imprisonment over physical punishment, reduced the number of capital offenses, and improved the conditions in jails. In 1790 the Walnut Street Jail in Philadelphia *(below)* was expanded and remodeled to meet these standards, making it the first prison in America.

Patent Medicine

Prior to the nineteenth century, most drugs were mixed by pharmacists, who made them by hand for each patient. When mass-produced, over-the-counter drugs became available in the mid-1800s, they often had secret and even dangerous ingredients. These types of drugs are now known as patent medicine, though very few were actually patented (legally protected). Patent medicines were made by all sorts of entrepreneurs, some without any medical training. The makers of these medicines claimed to cure such ailments as toothaches, paralysis, and even cancer. The medicines couldn't really cure disease, but they could relieve pain, due to the presence of drugs such as alcohol, cocaine, and opium. These drugs often caused the unknowing patients to develop dangerous addictions.

In the early part of the twentieth century, nearly every pharmacy had a soda fountain *(below)*, and pharmacists would mix sodas to cure physical complaints such as headaches. In the early days, some of these sodas contained dangerous drugs. This came to an end in 1914 with the passing of the Harrison Act, which banned the over-the-counter sale of cocaine and opiates. Many popular sodas such as Coca-Cola, 7Up, and Dr Pepper were first manufactured as patent medicines, but their ingredients are very different today.

The Black Cruise

In 1605 France established Port Royal in present-day Nova Scotia, Canada. This settlement was the start of a group of French territories that existed outside of Europe till the 1960s. These territories were known as the French Colonial Empire. In the early twentieth century, France possessed nearly 10 percent of the world's land area. Many of the French territories were in Africa.

In the 1920s, there were few roads in Africa. French colonists, industrialists, scientists, and the military wanted to create a link between mainland France and the African colonies. In 1924 Georges-Marie Haardt *(below center)*, Louis Audouin-Dubreuil *(below right)*, and a team of explorers attempted a journey across the entire continent of Africa. It took them 10 months to make the 17,000-mile trip. Their journey was called the Croisière Noire, or "Black Cruise." At the time, Africa was often called le continent noir, or "the Dark Continent," because it was mysterious and unknown to Europeans.

The expedition used eight half-track vehicles *(above)*, with regular wheels in front and a continuous track in the back, which allowed them to navigate the difficult terrain. The half-tracks were made by the French automobile manufacturer Citroën. While the Black Cruise was in part a publicity stunt for Citroën, it also had scientific endeavors. The explorers collected over 300 mammals, 800 birds, and 1,500 insects.

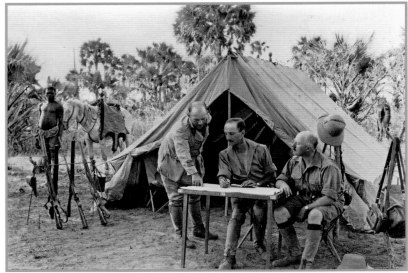

The Rain Forests of Iringa, Tanzania

Tanzania has a very diverse landscape. It is bordered by three of Africa's great lakes and is home to a number of active volcanoes including Mount Kilimanjaro, Africa's highest peak. Much of the country's interior is covered in sparse woodland and savannas. Lush rain forests cover the slope of the Eastern Arc, a chain of ancient mountains that stretches from southern Kenya to southern Tanzania. These mountains are sometimes called the Galapagos of Africa because they are home to flora and fauna that is endemic, or unique to a geographic region. Several species of tree-dwelling monkeys live in the Eastern Arc, including Iringa red colobuses. As their name implies, these endemic monkeys live in Iringa, the Tanzanian region that both Mortensen and the Black Cruise passed through.

Nazi Plunder

Adolf Hitler was a frustrated artist who was twice rejected from the Academy of Fine Arts Vienna. After he became Germany's chancellor in 1933, he orchestrated a campaign to confiscate valuable works of art. Hitler favored classic portraits and landscapes, especially those by the great masters of Germanic descent. He enforced his artistic ideals on Germany and labeled any artwork that didn't fit his ideals, such as modern art or art created by Communists or Jews, as *entartete kunst*, or "degenerate art."

During the war, the Nazis systematically removed hundreds of thousands of works of art from museums and private collections throughout Europe—the total plunder would exceed the collections at the Metropolitan Museum, the British Museum, and the Louvre combined. When the tide of the war changed, the Nazis tried to hide the artwork in unusual places such as salt mines, railroad cars, and abandoned castles. Many of the items were recovered by the Allied forces, but thousands of works are still missing.

Meteoroid, Meteor, or Meteorite?

STONY METEORITE

IRON METEORITE

STONY-IRON METEORITE

A meteoroid is a piece of debris found in the solar system. A meteoroid is larger than an atom but smaller than an asteroid. When meteoroids enter Earth's atmosphere at high velocity, the friction causes their surface to heat up and burn. This creates a visible streak in the sky that we call a meteor. If the meteoroid should survive its fall to Earth, it's called a meteorite.

There are three main categories of meteorite. The most common type is the stony meteorite, which is made of rocky material called silicate. Of the three types, stony meteorites are most similar to earth rocks in appearance and composition. Iron meteorites are made primarily of iron and nickel. Iron meteorites are easy to identify because they look and feel like metal. Sometimes their surface is covered with thumbprintlike indentations called regmaglypts, which are caused by the heat and erosion a meteoroid encounters when it travels through Earth's atmosphere. Stony-iron meteorites, the rarest of the three, consist of about equal parts silicate and iron-nickel. The pallasite, perhaps the most beautiful of all the meteorites, is a stony-iron meteorite with green-colored olivine crystals suspended in its metal body *(bottom left)*.

yn Chapman

12 by Graphic Universe™.

Jakobsen
Lerner Publishing Group, Inc.

Graphic Universe™
A division of Lerner Publishing Group, Inc.
241 First Avenue North
Minneapolis, MN 55401 U.S.A.

Website address: www.lernerbooks.com

Additional images in this book are used with the permission of: © Fototeca Storica Nazionale/Photodisc/Getty Images, p. 44 (left); © MPI/Stringer/Archive Photos/Getty Images, p. 44 (right); © The Power of Forever Photography/iStockphoto.com, p. 45 (left); Emil King, Minnesota Historical Society, p. 45 (right); © Photo12/The Image Works, p. 46 (top); © DR/adoc-photos/Art Resource, NY, p. 46 (bottom); © Adam Seward/Alamy, p. 47 (left); © William Vandivert/Time & Life Pictures/Getty Images, p. 47 (right); NASA, p. 48 (left top); © Emmanuel LATTES/Alamy, p. 48 (left center); © Detlev van Ravenswaay/Photo Researchers, Inc., p. 48 (left bottom); © Chad Baker/Photodisc/Getty Images, p. 48 (right).

Main body text set in CC Wild Words 7.5/8.
Typeface provided by Comicraft/Active Images.

Library of Congress Cataloging-in-Publication Data

Jakobsen, Lars, 1964-
     [Spjældet i Santa Fé. English]
     The Santa Fe jail / by Lars Jakobsen ; illustrated by Lars Jakobsen.
       p.   cm. — (Mortensen's escapades ; #02)
     Summary: While trying to ransom a scientist who was studying a rare metal, Mortensen is drugged and packed in a crate headed for Africa but soon learns that the scientist is wanted by more than one person, in more than one place and time.
     ISBN: 978-0-7613-7886-0 (lib. bdg. : alk. paper)
     1. Graphic novels [1. Graphic novels. 2. Time travel—Fiction. 3. Kidnapping—Fiction.] I. Title.
     PZ7.7.J648San 2012
     741.5'9489—dc23   2011044643

Manufactured in the United States of America
1 – CG – 7/15/12

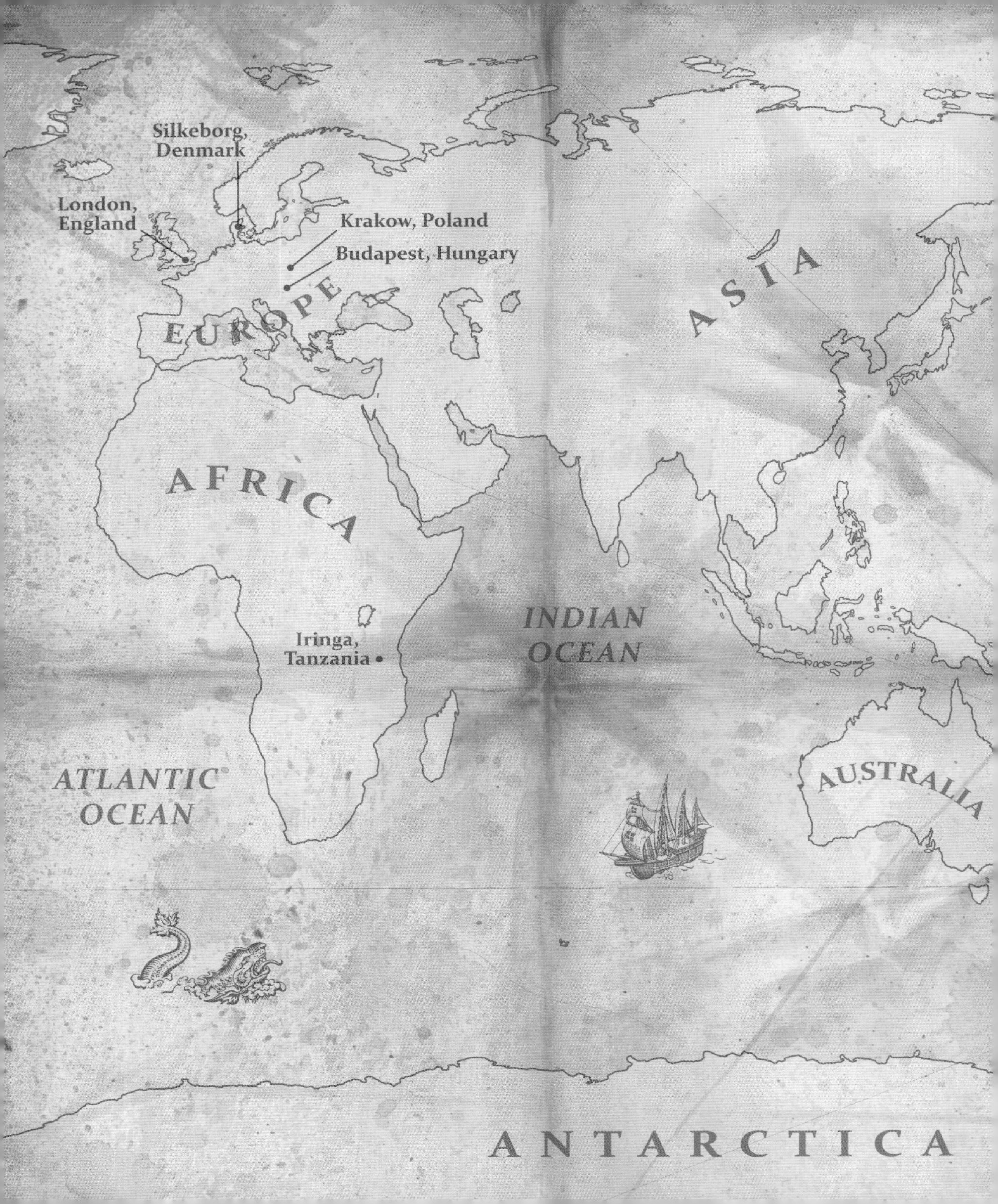

Silkeborg,
Denmark
London,
England
Krakow, Poland
Budapest, Hungary
EUROPE
ASIA
AFRICA
Iringa,
Tanzania
INDIAN
OCEAN
ATLANTIC
OCEAN
AUSTRALIA
ANTARCTICA